Goblin Soup

by Liza Charlesworth

ISBN: 978-1-338-78267-7
Illustrated by Raffaella Bolaffio
Copyright © 2021 by Liza Charlesworth. All rights reserved.
Published by Scholastic Inc., 557 Broadway, New York, NY 10012

10 9 8 7 6 5 4 3 2 1   68   21 22 23 24 25 26 27/0

Printed in Jiaxing, China. First printing, June 2021.

Should I put in cheese **or** rocks?

I will put in both!

Should I put in
pickles **or** socks?
I will put in both!

Should I put
worms **or** tape?
I will put in both!

5

Should I put
leaves **or** grapes?
I will put in both.

Should I in crayons **or** cake? I will put in both.

Mmmmmmmmmmmm!